RUNS WITH HORSES

≈≈≈≈≈≈≈

BRIAN BURKS

RUNS

WITH HORSES

SCHOLASTIC INC.

New York   Toronto   London   Auckland   Sydney

ISBN 0-590-93254-3

12 11 10 9 8 7 6 5 4 3 2 1   6 7 8 9/9 0 1/0

Printed in the U.S.A.   01

First Scholastic printing, October 1996

For the cold, snowy day at the ranch in White Oaks, when only the flicker of a dream remained, and you kindled the fire.

"Until I was about ten years old I did not know that people died except by violence. That is because I am an Apache."

—James Kaywaykla
1877–1963

PROLOGUE

The year was 1886. After breaking out of the Fort Apache reservation in Arizona a year earlier, Geronimo and Chief Naiche led a small band of Chiricahua Apaches into the rugged terrain of Mexico's Sierra Madre.

There, for a while, they would be safe from the pursuit of the United States Army and free to raid the Mexicans for much needed supplies. The months in hiding, the remoteness of their location, and the raids allowed them to train boys to become warriors, something Geronimo was always short of.

Runs With Horses sat on the ground across from his father, waiting patiently for the short, compact man to speak. At last, as the gray light of dawn began to erase the stars from the sky, Red Knife raised his head and parted his long black hair from his wide, flat, sun-hardened face.

"My son, you are not yet a Chiricahua Apache warrior. You have been on two raids, but you must go on two more before you can take your place at the fire with the men. There is still much to learn.

"You know that in this world no one will help you, not even me. Your legs are your friends. You must teach them to run like the antelope. Then your enemies will not be able to catch you.

"Your eyes are your friends. You must make them see like the eagle so that you are a great hunter and your enemies cannot approach without your knowledge.

"Your ears are your friends. They will tell you what your eyes cannot see in the night. Teach them to hear the beetle that crawls on the ground. Then you will hear the snake slither in the grass and it will not be able to bite you.

"Your arms and your hands are your friends. They must be strong and quick like the cougar's."

Red Knife pointed to his forehead. "Your mind is your friend. It will tell you what to do. Remember all that you hear and see. In your head will be the wisdom to survive all things.

"Someday your people will be hungry. You will have to kill your enemy and steal something for your people to eat. Then all the camps will talk about you. They will say that my son is a great warrior. Do you understand these things I have told you?"

Runs With Horses nodded solemnly and they both stood. Red Knife gestured to the edge of the camp at the silhouette of a lone brave standing in a small clearing, his arms folded against his chest. "It is time. Stands Alone is there waiting for you. You will go."

Runs With Horses moved beside Stands Alone, the young unmarried warrior who was to accompany him. Like the man, he wore only a broad loincloth made of buckskin, which fell in front to just above his knees and hung low in back only high enough that he couldn't step on it.

A sheath holding a knife was attached to the rawhide belt around his waist and his knee-high moccasins were rolled down to the ankles. A tight, apprehensive feeling grew in his stomach as the brave stooped to lift a water jug from the ground beside them. Could he do it? Could he run the three miles to the top of the mountain and then back without swallowing or spitting out the mouthful of water?

The pitch-lined basket of water was put to his lips and he filled his mouth, then pulled his long black hair to the back and adjusted his brow band. A moment later Stands Alone shouted.

"Go!"

Runs With Horses was tall for an Apache and he moved out swiftly.

His training for the task ahead of him had begun when he was seven. Every morning for nine years, he'd gotten up before daylight and run, keeping his mouth closed, breathing only through his nose. He was ready for this test. Still, the fear of failure gripped him. If he tripped and fell, it would be hard to keep from swallowing the water.

The treacherous terrain of the Sierra Madre made the run difficult. The novice warrior dodged or jumped boulders, deep arroyos, and cactus and thorny mesquite bushes, which threatened to rip his flesh with the miss of a step.

Stands Alone ran with him to make sure he went to the top of the peak before turning back. The brave stayed far to the side, allowing each of them room to choose their own way.

Runs With Horses glanced at Stands Alone and marveled at the ease with which the man seemed to float across the ground. He wondered if he looked the same, or if his stride was awkward and rough in comparison.

He knew the steepest part of the mountain was not far ahead, the part that would try to pull the power from his legs and the wind from his lungs.

Runs With Horses thought back. It was night, and a thin layer of ice covered the deep pool into which his father told him to dive. The ice cut and scraped his skin. The frigid water numbed him. After he managed to swim to the bank and worm his way up it, he wasn't allowed near the fire. He was forced to stay outside the camp until daybreak, covering his naked body with soil, leaves, and pine needles to keep from freezing to death. An Apache warrior must be able to survive any hardship, his father had said.

The following day he was told to fight a tree, and when his hands were bloody and swollen he had to roll a ball of snow until the ball became too big and heavy to be pushed. Later that evening, dry sage was placed on both his forearms and allowed to burn to ashes. He did not flinch or close his eyes. A warrior must be able to stand pain. The scars still showed on his arms.

Suddenly, at the realization that this run was but one of many trials he'd faced on his journey to adulthood, he relaxed and shifted the water in his mouth. There would be more training, some of it dangerous.

≈≈≈

Runs With Horses heard the faint buzz of a rattlesnake and out of the corner of his eye saw the blurred flash of the snake's strike. In the middle of his stride, he twisted and threw his weight forward, at the same time bringing his knees to his chest. The strike missed and he unfolded his body, landing on his feet well ahead of the snake. It had been close, he knew, very close.

Higher up, piñon and cedar trees became more numerous, adding still more obstacles to Runs With Horses' path. He was not allowed to slow down. If Stands Alone saw him trotting or walking, the test was over and it might be weeks before he'd get the chance to try again.

The steep part of the run started. Sweat drenched Runs With Horses' brow band and trickled down his face, stinging his eyes. The muscles in his legs tightened and the air rushing in and out of his nostrils burned his dry throat. Stands Alone was still with him, not far to the side, watching him.

His now almost vertical route lay between two large boulders. The top of an ancient, gnarled juniper grew overhead and its fallen needles covered the ground below it. Runs With Horses didn't see the exposed root across his way. It snagged the toes of his left foot and tripped him. He frantically tried to regain his feet and keep his momentum from throwing him headfirst to the ground.

He fell.

Water went down his throat. But only a little of it. The run wasn't over. The prayers of the shaman had closed his throat and helped him. He scrambled to his feet and resumed his punishing pace.

When the top of the peak was in sight, his heaving lungs seemed ready to burst and his body trembled with weakness. His father's words echoed through his mind. "You must know that you can beat your enemy. There must not be any doubt."

The peak above became the enemy. Runs

With Horses forced his legs faster and faster. His eyes were glued to the ground, so he did not notice that he'd left Stands Alone far behind. Everything in him was focused on his task.

He reached the top and spun on his heels to start back, taking no time to relish the defeat of the peak. Real victory was three miles away at camp.

The descent was easier, though the chances of stumbling and falling were greater. A line of mesquites barred the way ahead and he lengthened his steps and leaped, rising nearly shoulder height in the air.

As his right leg grazed the top of one of the bushes, thorns ripped the skin open. He landed on the other side in a shallow gully. The uneven sandy footing caused him to falter, but he charged up the opposite bank, straightening his body as he went.

Further along, the slope gentled and an unexpected freshness came over Runs With Horses. He liked the wind in his face and the way his feet barely touched the ground with each stride. He was no longer human, he was an antelope, and he pushed himself faster.

When the camp finally came into view, Runs With Horses felt like he was flying. He stopped in front of his waiting father. Red Knife was pleased to see the sweat covering his son's lithe body. Geronimo, a stocky, dark-faced man with a broad, heavy nose, low forehead, and eyes as black as obsidian, walked up.

"Spit," he demanded.

Runs With Horses turned his head and a stream of water shot from between his lips. He smiled and opened his mouth to help catch his breath.

"Where is the brave who went with you?" Red Knife asked.

Runs With Horses shook his head. "I do not know."

When a short while later Stands Alone trotted in, Geronimo's thin mouth tightened into a straight line. He was not happy. The war leader and medicine man took all the boys' training very seriously.

"Why weren't you with him?" he snapped, pointing at Runs With Horses.

The warrior looked down. "The boy runs like the deer. His feet are sure like the mountain goat. I could not keep up."

"Did he go to the top?"

Stands Alone met Geronimo's glare. "He did. I saw him."

Red Knife and Geronimo turned and walked away. Runs With Horses grinned. Victory was sweet.

Runs With Horses sat on the ground across from his father. The morning sun had not yet appeared above the mountains to the east.

"My son," Red Knife began, "when you were small and did not know how to make a bow and arrow, I made them for you. I showed you how to hunt. I told you that the birds and squirrels and rabbits were not tame. When they see you, the birds fly away and the squirrels and rabbits run and hide. You must see them before they see you. You must creep and get close to your game, so your arrow can hit them.

"In hunting small animals, you have learned that you must go very slowly and softly, not rattling the stones with your feet or making any rocks roll down a steep place. To hunt deer, it is the same. You must go slyly and carefully. Deer can see you before you see them. The deer stays where he can see very well. You will have to look for him and go up to him like the fox. It is the same with the antelope and other animals. But do not hunt the turkey. They are no good for food because they eat insects."

Red Knife paused before continuing. "Today you will leave here, alone, with your fire drill, knife, your bow and your arrows. Do not return without a deer or an antelope. A warrior must be able to hunt and provide meat for his people.

"Do not eat before you leave or take any food with you. If you hunt on an empty stomach, Life Giver might take pity on you and provide you with a deer. Be sure to ask the crow to help you. When you make your kill, mark the tips of your moccasins with the blood and eat the heart raw as quickly as you can to insure continued success in hunting.

"Now go."

Runs With Horses stopped at the edge of camp to examine his weapon. He'd made the single curved bow from the branch of a mulberry tree. It was the same length as two arrows and was strung with the tendons of a deer his father had killed. He carried an extra string in his quiver.

Finding no flaws in the bow, he laid it down, then removed the quiver from across his back and examined each of his twelve arrows. The shafts were made from mountain mahogany, peeled, scraped, and allowed to dry. Under his father's directions, he'd straightened them against a heated rock, then painted bands on them with the hues extracted from boiled roots and tree bark. The flint arrowheads he'd found were made by the Pueblo Indians centuries ago and the feathers at the opposite end of the shaft came from the tail of an eagle.

Satisfied, Runs With Horses set off at an easy trot. He knew where he was going. There was a narrow box canyon many miles to the west and a little north. A seep spring was in the bottom of it. Red Knife had taken him there once, months ago, and he hoped he could remember the way. It was a good place to hunt because game came from miles around to drink when there had been no rain, and it hadn't rained in a long time.

A crow cawed overhead and Runs With Horses stopped to watch the black bird. He spoke to it. "Crow, I am hunting. If I kill a deer or antelope you will get the entrails, so you should help me."

The bird circled once more and flew west. Runs With Horses took this as a sign that he was going to the right place. His pace quickened. He knew that a strong warrior could cover seventy miles a day on foot. The miles of rugged country ahead of him were an easy half day's jaunt.

Tirelessly he jogged on, constantly scanning the land around him for anything peculiar that might be an enemy. From the many stories he'd heard around camp, his people had always had enemies.

The first were the Plains Indians and the Pueblos. Later came the Spaniards, who seized hundreds of Apaches and forced them to work as slaves in the mines. Now the enemies were the Mexicans and the newcomers across the border to the north, the White Eyes.

Leaders of the once powerful Apache Nation, such as Victorio, Mangas Coloradas, and Naiche's father, Cochise, were either imprisoned on the White Eyes' reservations, or were dead. Chief Naiche, Geronimo, and their followers were the last holdouts.

≈≈≈

Runs With Horses tried to keep his route in the bottoms of canyons or through thick brush, staying as much as possible away from the flats, where he could be seen for long distances. If he was spotted by the Mexicans and they caught him, they would kill him.

As he traveled, a jackrabbit or cottontail occasionally jumped from its resting place in the shade of a rock or bush. In one deep draw he glimpsed the white tail of a deer bouncing ahead of him. He paid it little attention. Runs With Horses knew that it was useless to follow a spooked deer. He would never get close enough to it for a shot.

Before midday he reached the box canyon, surprised at how easily he'd remembered the way. He dropped to his stomach and crawled to the edge of the rocky rim to look down. Where there is water, his father had told him, there is danger. Enemies could be around.

The hot summer sun was now high in the sky and it gleamed on the water below. Runs With Horses carefully scanned the canyon for any movement.

Assured that no one was there, he rose and followed a faint ribbon of a trail that zigzagged back and forth down the steep canyon wall. Fresh deer tracks in the powdery dirt told him the trail was a good place for an ambush. He looked for a spot nearby where he could hide and the breeze would not carry his scent to his quarry.

Close to the bottom of the canyon, he found it—a deep ravine running crossways to the trail with a short, bushy cedar tree at the head of it. He silently inched his way down the bank and knelt behind the tree.

In a moment he stood, pulling back an arrow notched in the string of his bow. His view was good and the distance to the trail close. He smiled as he lowered the bow and returned the arrow to his quiver. The site was perfect. He didn't see how he could miss.

Following the gravelly bed of the ravine down to a pool fed by the seep spring, Runs With Horses looked for tracks in the mud to find out if anyone had recently been there. Finding none, he drank his fill of the briny water and returned to the ambush site to wait out the day. It would be late evening before the deer would come down the trail to water. In the meantime, he'd stay in the shade of the cedar and rest.

The midday hours passed slowly. Finally, part of the sun sank below the western horizon and Runs With Horses sat up and made his bow ready, then watched the trail through an opening in the branches. He was hungry—and glad of it. The Giver of Life had the power to provide all things, including a fat buck.

A shadow swept by on the ground and he looked up to see a crow circling. He was sure it was the same crow he'd spoken to earlier and its presence increased his anticipation. The dusk light was rapidly fading when he heard a noise above him. The sound of small hooves striking the ground grew louder and clearer.

The gray of two deer appeared in the trail. Runs With Horses trembled in excitement. He knew he had very little time to shoot, knew he should let his already aimed arrow fly to-ward the heart of the doe, standing closest to him.

But he wanted the buck, wanted the horns to proudly show his father and Geronimo. He shifted his aim. The buck was a much harder shot.

It was a mistake.

Just as he released the arrow, both deer bolted and ran wildly up the steep canyon wall in a cloud of dust. The spent arrow clattered harmlessly against some rocks.

Runs With Horses stared at the empty trail, ashamed and depressed. The Giver of Life and the crow had helped him, had made his task easy, and he'd failed them.

No warrior would have been so stupid. Doe meat was no different from that of a buck, and meat was what he was after, not horns. A long night on an empty stomach now lay ahead of him and tomorrow he could expect no help or pity from Life Giver or Crow. He was on his own.

After finding his broken-tipped arrow, he made his way down to the water, washed his face, and drank. Then he moved a short way back up the ravine to spend the night where the light from his fire could not be easily seen.

There was no reason for him to build a fire; it wasn't cold and he had nothing to cook, but he wanted one. It might be hours before sleep came, and the flames would keep him company.

He picked a soft, sandy spot, gathered a few dead twigs and limbs from a mesquite along with some dry grass, and removed the fire drill from his belt. The drill was made up of two pieces of wood: one a juniper stick ten inches long and about the thickness of his little finger, the other a thin, flat piece of yucca.

Runs With Horses placed the blunt end of the juniper stick into a notch in the center of the yucca, gathered some of the grass around it, and quickly rotated the stick between his palms.

Unable to get a spark or smoke, he put a pinch of sand in the notch and tried again. This time a thin plume of smoke rose. He removed the juniper stick, pressed the grass against the notch in the yucca wood, and blew on it. In a moment the grass was ablaze and he added the twigs.

The night darkness was complete. An owl

hooted nearby. A shiver crept down Runs With Horses' back and he was grateful for the light of the fire. The owl's presence meant someone evil had died in the vicinity and his or her spirit had entered the owl. "Nothing good ever comes from the presence of an owl," Red Knife had told him. "Only sickness and death."

The owl hooted again and again and in a few minutes Runs With Horses could stand no more. He grabbed a burning limb out of the fire and ran in the direction of the bird.

When he heard the sound of flapping wings, he stopped, grateful that the big bird had left. He hoped that it wouldn't return. He did not want to die.

Hours later, after recounting his earlier mistakes with the deer dozens of times and asking the Giver of Life and the crow to forgive him, Runs With Horses went to sleep.

The night was still black when he awoke and he immediately searched the eastern sky for the morning star, knowing that no warrior allows the star to get up before he does. The star wasn't there, but it would be soon. His instinct told him that.

He lay still. He wanted to go to the pool of water and drink but knew he would make too much noise in the darkness. It would not be wise to scare away any deer or antelope that might be around. The thought of stepping on or near a rattlesnake also kept him still, waiting for the morning light.

When dawn arrived, Runs With Horses had to make a decision. Should he slip quietly down to the water, hoping to find a deer there within arrow range, or should he go back to yesterday evening's ambush site at the head of the ravine and wait?

From the tracks he'd seen in the trail, deer used it both to come into the canyon and to go back out. Chances were good that any deer now at the water would use the trail to climb out of the canyon. He decided to try the ambush site one more time.

Runs With Horses was ready when he heard a deer approaching him from below. This time, he assured himself, he would make no mistakes. For years he'd hunted squirrels, birds, rabbits, and pack rats, which were much harder to hit than a deer. He was confident of his shooting ability.

The deer came closer and he drew his notched arrow back. A moment later, looking through the branches of the cedar, he saw the deer's head. It was a buck, a much larger buck than the one he'd seen yesterday. Runs With Horses started shaking and he felt weak. *No,* he thought. *Unless the deer offers a perfect shot, I will not shoot.*

The buck took a few more steps. Runs With Horses knew there wouldn't be a better chance, not even from a doe or yearling fawn. His thoughts stopped.

Ever so slowly he raised up above the scrub cedar and aimed behind the deer's front shoulder. The buck halted and turned his head. Runs With Horses released his arrow and the twang of the string was loud in the stillness.

Runs With Horses saw the arrow hit the mark and bury itself deep in the deer's flesh. The buck lunged forward and ran. Runs With Horses couldn't contain his excitement. He let out a shrill yell and dashed after the wounded animal.

It was all wrong. He knew better. "Be quiet and wait after shooting an animal so that it will get sick and lie down," Red Knife had told him many times. "An animal will get strength from its fright and will go much further than if it is left alone."

But the buck didn't go far, couldn't go far. The arrow had pierced his lungs. Runs With Horses saw the deer stagger, then fall. When he reached the animal, he pulled out his knife and slashed the deer's throat, allowing the blood to drain from the carcass.

He had never been happier and he silently thanked the Giver of Life for putting the deer here for the Apache to eat.

Runs With Horses grabbed the horns and dragged the heavy buck around until the head was to the east. This was important because one of the creators, Child of Water, had done this when he hunted upon the earth.

Being careful not to straddle the deer or ever step in front of the head, Runs With Horses removed the arrow with several hard jerks. He then slit the deer open with his knife and removed the entrails as he'd helped his father do many times before.

He remembered Red Knife's words about the heart. Taking it in both hands, Runs With Horses ate it, wiping the dripping blood off his chin and placing it on the tips of his moccasins. It was essential that he have continued success in hunting. Someday, after he became a warrior, he hoped to have a wife and family. He would need to provide for them.

A crow cawed above and Runs With Horses stood up. He pointed at the deer. "Crow, you have helped me. We are friends. You and I will not be hungry. The entrails are yours."

He looked at the deer. "Deer, don't be afraid when we see each other again. I need your meat and your skin. May I always have good luck with you."

Runs With Horses left the deer and went down to the canyon to drink. He soon returned, made a fire, and roasted some of the meat. After he'd eaten his fill, he finished butchering the buck.

Unable to carry all the meat, he placed half of it in the hide, forming a tight bundle, and hung it up in a nearby cedar with string he'd made from the leaf of a yucca. The bundle was high enough that a coyote or bobcat couldn't reach it.

He spoke to all the animals. "This meat belongs to the Giver of Life. It must not be touched. I will return for it."

Runs With Horses put his bow over his shoulder and picked up the deer's head and hindquarters. It was a heavy load. Red Knife and Geronimo would be proud of him.

Geronimo walked up and stood in front of Red Knife and Runs With Horses, who sat beside a fire in front of their wickiup. Runs With Horses stood and moved to the side.

Geronimo pointed at him while looking at Red Knife. "You have a good boy. There is another boy in camp who is better, quicker, and stronger."

Red Knife's sober expression didn't change. His gaze was direct and his voice emotionless. "It will be light soon. Bring the boy here. Tell the camp to come and watch. I want everyone to see it."

After Geronimo was out of sight, Runs With Horses resumed his position by the fire. He'd listened to the conversation and knew what was going to happen. It had happened twice before and both times he'd hated it, although he'd won.

There were only a few boys in the camp close to his age and almost all of them were his friends. This was one part of warrior training he wished he could avoid.

Red Knife sensed his son's sadness.

"My son, how can an eagle fly if he never spreads his wings? How does the lion know he can catch and kill a deer if he has never done it? It is the same for you.

"The day is soon coming when your training will be over. The games will end and the struggle will be for life or death, not only for yourself but for your people. You must know your strengths and weaknesses, just as your opponent must know his. A coward is no good to himself or anyone else."

The last statement sparked anger in Runs With Horses and he did something he'd never done before. He talked back to his father.

"I am not afraid. You should not speak to me in this way. The others are my friends. I grew up playing with them, swimming and hunting with them. They are not my enemies."

Red Knife smiled and his brown eyes were warm. Although he tried never to let it show, he loved Runs With Horses more than anything in the world.

"Your heart is good, it is pure," he said quietly. "But if this boy is your friend, you will show him how slow he is. You will show him how weak he is. You will give him no mercy and he will work harder, hoping to someday beat you.

"The abilities you force him to sharpen will someday save his life and the lives of others. Do you understand what I am telling you?"

Runs With Horses nodded, staring at the flames. His father's words made sense but didn't change his mind. He still didn't like the idea of trying to hurt his friends. He didn't like it at all.

≈≈≈

Everyone in the camp was there, forming a large circle on a piece of open, level land. The people cheered as Runs With Horses' heart sank. Geronimo entered the circle with Little Face beside him. Little Face was more than a friend. He was like a brother. Geronimo knew that, and so did Red Knife.

The boys met in the center of the ring. Runs With Horses could see the fear, the quiet pleading in Little Face's eyes. The two had wrestled each other in fun many times before and Little Face always lost. He was smaller than Runs With Horses; perhaps quicker, but no match in strength.

Geronimo handed each of them a stick, then stepped back. "You will fight until one of you says 'enough.' Do not give up easily or your training will be stopped. I will not take you on the next raid.

"Begin!"

The boys crouched low and began to circle each other. They knew the implications of what Geronimo had said. It might be as long as a year before either of them was allowed to resume his training. They wouldn't be considered for the next raid, and without the raids, they'd never become warriors, never be thought of as adults or be allowed to smoke or to marry. Besides, no Apache girl worth having would show any interest in them.

Runs With Horses' thoughts raced. He knew the damage and pain the sticks could cause. After his last fight he'd been so sore he could hardly move for a week. His opponent had fared worse, with a broken wrist, nose, and finger.

Suddenly Runs With Horses dropped his stick and dove at Little Face's feet. If he could turn the fight into a wrestling match, there was little chance that either of them would be hurt seriously.

Little Face swung his stick viciously, hitting Runs With Horses on the back, causing him to flinch against the pain and barely manage to grab one foot. Again and again Little Face hit him, once on the back of his head.

The blows hurt Runs With Horses, causing fierce, uncontrollable rage. He'd dropped his stick to keep from harming his friend, and that friend was beating him mercilessly.

The circle of people yelled and moaned, some chanted his name, but Runs With Horses stopped hearing. Adrenaline rushed through his veins and he gathered his strength while Little Face continued to strike him.

With the agility of a cat, Runs With Horses sprang up, bringing Little Face's foot with him. Little Face was thrown off balance and he slammed hard against the ground.

Runs With Horses quickly scrambled on top of his friend who had suddenly become his enemy. Little Face raised the stick and Runs With Horses grabbed it, easily twisting it out of his hand.

Anger continued to control Runs With Horses' actions. He pinned Little Face's arms with his knees and put the stick across the boy's throat, pushing down on the ends with all his might. Little Face's eyes bugged out and he gasped for air. He struggled and kicked but could not break Runs With Horses' hold.

Little Face coughed and gagged.

The people grew silent. Geronimo and Red Knife moved beside Runs With Horses and forcefully raised him up. Little Face curled up on his side, gulping air.

Red Knife slapped his son on the back and smiled. It was then that Runs With Horses' angry trance broke and he realized what he'd done. He'd almost killed Little Face.

Red Knife's voice was loud. "This is my son. I am proud of him. You have all seen what he can do. He will be a mighty warrior."

The people cheered. Runs With Horses wiped his brow with his forearm and brought it down, noticing streaks of blood on it. He dropped the stick and knelt beside Little Face. He didn't feel like a hero. He felt like a fool, a fool who had let his anger get completely out of control.

What if Geronimo and his father hadn't stopped him? Little Face would be dead.

The noon sun was bright. Runs With Horses was doing the thing that had given him his name. He was staying with the horses. Whenever anyone wanted to find him, they knew where to look, for he was rarely far from the large, muscular animals.

The horses intrigued him and he never tired of watching them, talking to them. He was certain they understood what he said. But today he paid them little attention. His thoughts were on his mother, who had died giving birth to his stillborn brother. Her name, Stepping

On Water, had not been spoken since her death nine years ago.

It was the way of the Apaches. Talking or thinking about the dead only made one sad, and worse, it might bring back their ghost. Runs With Horses knew the danger—and didn't want to be haunted by a ghost—but he couldn't help it. He missed his mother, missed her big brown eyes, crooked smile, and soft, soothing voice.

Her burial took place the same day she died and Runs With Horses remembered every detail of it: the wails of the people and the tears streaming down his father's face.

At the end of that bleak day, everything that had belonged to her—everything she had used, including pots and baskets—had been either buried with her or burned.

Before sundown, Runs With Horses had watched his father kill his mother's spotted pony, then set fire to their dome-shaped brush wickiup. The following day the camp was moved. Nothing remained that would remind anyone of Stepping On Water.

But the grave and the fire couldn't erase the memories. Red Knife had never really gotten over her death, Runs With Horses knew. The man wouldn't consider marrying again and he drank too much tiswin. And he wasn't happy, not like before.

Runs With Horses heard a noise behind him and turned to see Little Face approaching. He stood up. He hadn't seen Little Face since their fight three days ago.

Little Face stopped several feet away. "I knew I would find you here."

Runs With Horses stared at the purplish yellow bruise on Little Face's throat, then looked at the ground. "I'm sorry about the other day. I was angry. I did not know what I was doing."

"It is all right. When you dropped your stick, I should have dropped mine, but for once I thought I might beat you."

Runs With Horses sat back down. He motioned for Little Face to sit beside him. "Why have you come?"

"To warn you. Two warriors came into camp with some bottles of mescal they stole from the Mexicans. Chief Naiche, Geronimo, your father, and two or three others are drinking it. They are already drunk."

Runs With Horses shrugged. Whenever there was something strong to drink, the men drank it.

Little Face continued. "Red Knife is making bets on you. He says you can ride any wild horse bareback without a rope. He is betting his rifle against more of the mescal."

"His rifle?" Runs With Horses knew what a gun was worth, and how hard it was to get. Only warriors—but not all—had them. His father's lever-action repeating Winchester had come from a raid on white settlers to the north. Most of the other men in camp had only single-shot Springfield carbines. The Winchester was worth two or three good horses, and a horse was also very hard to get.

A shiver ran down Runs With Horses' spine. There was a lot at stake. He was sure of his riding ability, having spent years training under his father's directions and having been to a shaman who had performed a ceremony to give him the clinging ability of the bat. It was said around camp that he had "the power" with horses.

But to ride a wild, bucking horse without a rope was something he'd never attempted. It was crazy, maybe even impossible.

Runs With Horses stood. "The bet will not matter if they cannot find me. Tomorrow or the next day the drink will wear off and they will forget about it. I will go hide."

Little Face nodded. But as Runs With Horses started to leave, he saw his father and a group of men approaching him.

The thought to run and keep on running flashed through his mind. They likely hadn't seen him yet, but Runs With Horses couldn't do it. If he was seen running away, it would bring shame to his father and he couldn't chance that.

Little Face stepped beside him, seeming to understand. "Do not worry. We have ridden together many times. I know that no one rides better than you. I have an eagle's feather and I will get it. We will tie it to the mane of the horse they choose and it will help to calm him."

Runs With Horses turned to Little Face. "It is good we are still friends."

Little Face nodded and left to get the feather.

≈≈≈

Red Knife laid his hand on Runs With Horses' shoulder. The smell of mescal was strong on his breath, his speech was slurred, and his eyes were red and dull.

"My son. These"—he gestured at the others with him—"these men say you cannot ride a horse with no rope. I know"—he staggered—"I know that you can. You will show them."

Runs With Horses was silent. There was nothing to say. He wouldn't argue with his father, especially not in front of the other men.

Red Knife turned to the tallest of the men—slender and rawboned. "Naiche, you pick the horse."

The group of men moved closer to the hobbled horses. Runs With Horses stayed where he was and listened to them talk about which horse would be the hardest to ride. He already knew.

There were three two-year-old colts in the bunch that had never been ridden or handled. The horses were stolen on the last raid to Frontera, a small Mexican settlement to the north.

Of the three colts, a short-backed blue roan with rounded withers and white in his eyes would give the most trouble. The horse didn't like people and even Runs With Horses hadn't been able to get very close to him.

Little Face returned with the feather. Naiche had made up his mind. It would be the blue roan. Stands Alone, the warrior who had accompanied Runs With Horses on his run to the top of the peak, took a rawhide rope from around his shoulder and after considerable difficulty managed to lasso the hobbled horse.

The other men, as well as their drunken state would permit, helped hold the animal. Red Knife took off his shirt and used it to blindfold the horse while Geronimo removed the hobbles.

Runs With Horses stepped beside the roan. His insides were so tight they hurt. Except for Little Face, no one had mentioned the bet and Runs With Horses found himself wishing he didn't know about it. Then, at least, the pressure wouldn't be so great.

Little Face tied the feather on the colt with strands of hair from the mane and stepped back. Runs With Horses knew that waiting would only make his anxiety worse. The ride was ahead of him and there was no way out of it.

He grabbed a handful of the colt's mane and swung aboard. Red Knife jerked the blindfold off and the blue roan lunged forward, knocking the man down.

The other men doubled over, laughing at Red Knife. The colt reared up, tottering back and forth on his hind legs. Runs With Horses clung to the mane with both hands, hoping the horse wouldn't fall over backward and crush him. If he let go, his father would lose the rifle.

At last the roan's front hooves returned to the ground and he jumped in a high arch, coming down with a jolt that caused Runs With Horses to lose his balance. The eagle feather might work on some horses, but it didn't seem to have any effect on this one.

Runs With Horses struggled to pull himself back to the center of the roan's back. The horse bolted into a full gallop and Runs With Horses was glad. A straight run was easy to ride and it would help to tire the animal out.

The open flats of the mountain tabletop lay in front of them. The colt picked up speed. Ahead, Runs With Horses knew, was a sheer drop-off where the mesa ended. If the young horse didn't stop or change direction, neither of them would live through that fall.

Runs With Horses leaned as far forward as he could on the animal's neck, trying desperately to reach the colt's nose. If he was able to get hold of it, get his fingers up one of the nostrils, he might then force the horse to turn or stop.

But the roan wouldn't allow it. He stretched his neck out and kept his nose just out of reach. Runs With Horses glanced ahead. There was no more time.

He was bracing himself to bail off when the colt slid to an abrupt stop. The force of the move was too great, too unexpected. Runs With Horses' hands were torn from the mane and he flew over the horse's head, slamming against the ground, then tumbling within inches of the edge of the sheer drop-off.

Gasping for the air that had been knocked from him, he watched through blurred eyes as the roan turned and trotted off in the direction of the other horses. He'd lost. His father would lose the Winchester.

Runs With Horses started walking. Soon he saw Little Face coming toward him on a blaze-faced sorrel. The boy stopped the horse along-side him.

"Don't be sad," Little Face said. "It is not your fault. Red Knife is drunk. He is to blame. He—"

"No," Runs With Horses almost shouted. "You will not speak against my father."

Little Face shrugged and put his hand out. Runs With Horses grabbed his friend's arm and swung on behind him. Soon they were back with the horses, the blue roan grazing contentedly among them as if nothing unusual had happened.

Runs With Horses looked toward camp and saw the men walking in the distance, his father lagging behind the others. Red Knife stopped and looked back a moment, then moved on. Runs With Horses could tell the man was disappointed, and that bothered him.

A week passed and though Red Knife hadn't mentioned it, the loss of the rifle continued to trouble Runs With Horses.

It wasn't so much that he considered the loss his fault. Few men, if any, could have ridden the roan without a rope. But the right or wrong of it didn't matter—the rifle was gone and Red Knife needed it.

Little Face aimed a little higher than the horizon and released the arrow.

Runs With Horses stepped up and watched until the arrow fell. He shook his head. "It did not go far enough. My arrow is farther."

"No." Little Face shook his head. "My arrow went farther."

The two trotted across the open flat, the same place where the blue roan had bolted with Runs With Horses. Little Face found his arrow first, then, a little farther, Runs With Horses found his. Little Face reluctantly handed over his arrow.

"You have won three of my arrows. We will go and shoot at the bluff."

Runs With Horses smiled. He and Little Face had played these games since they were little. In the end neither of them ever won many more arrows than the other.

They reached a wide draw north of the camp. On one side was a high bank of soft red dirt. Little Face looked at Runs With Horses. "You have more arrows than I do. You shoot first."

Runs With Horses looked through his quiver and picked out his worst arrow. The shaft was bent and some feathers were missing. If he lost it, it wouldn't matter too much.

He pulled his bow taut and shot the arrow into the bank. Little Face grinned. He could tell by the way the arrow flew that it was no good.

"So, you are afraid I will win?"

"We will see." Runs With Horses shrugged.

Little Face notched his best arrow in the string. He took careful aim and let it fly. The shot went true and the arrow half buried itself in the soft dirt beside Runs With Horses' arrow. Little Face ran to see if the shafts were touching. They were.

"I won!" Little Face shouted. "Come look."

"No, I believe you. Take it."

Runs With Horses searched his quiver for his next-worst arrow and shot it into the bank. Little Face aimed carefully and shot again, but this time the arrow shafts didn't touch. It was now his turn to shoot into the bank and he used the same bent arrow he'd just won from Runs With Horses.

Red Knife walked up and both boys turned to him. Little Face offered his bow. "Will you shoot with us?"

The man smiled and took the bow. He and Little Face's father, Broken Foot, had spent a lot of time together teaching the boys to hunt and to shoot. But since Broken Foot was killed while stealing cattle in New Mexico Territory two years ago, Red Knife had spent less time with the boys.

He took three arrows from Little Face's quiver, notched one in the bowstring, and carefully positioned the other two between the fingers of his left hand.

Quickly he raised the bow and sent the notched arrow skyward. Before the arrow returned to the ground, he shot the other two arrows into the dirt bank, putting them so close together that they appeared as one.

Runs With Horses was surprised. He'd never seen his father do that before. He knew the man could shoot, but not that well.

Red Knife handed the bow back to Little Face.

"This will be your new game. A warrior should be able to do it. If you do not shoot twice before the first arrow falls, you lose an arrow. If the two arrows in the bluff do not touch, you lose an arrow."

He turned to leave. "Come, both of you."

Little Face retrieved his arrows and the boys followed Red Knife. Not far from camp, in an area covered with stones, they found Stands

Alone waiting for them. The young warrior handed each of them a sling and kept one for himself.

Red Knife spoke, pointing to one side of a narrow, shallow gully. "You will go there."

He pointed to the other side. "We will go there. We will sling stones at each other. If a stone hits you, it might break a bone. If it hits you in the head, you are gone. This will make you quick, make you be able to dodge and to duck like the fish that swims in the river."

Runs With Horses and Little Face laid their bows and quivers down and slowly walked to the side Red Knife had pointed to. They both knew the seriousness of the training ahead. More than once they'd seen boys who had gone through this training return to camp with broken arms and ribs. One time a rock had knocked a boy's eye out and it was said that years ago a boy had been killed.

Red Knife and Stands Alone each picked up a stone and positioned it in the rawhide bottoms of their slings. The boys did the same. Red Knife twirled his sling above his head, slowly at first, then faster, while gluing his eyes to his son.

Runs With Horses met his father's gaze,

knowing that the man was serious and this was no game. He reluctantly started to twirl his own sling, the rawhide strings familiar in his hand. He and Little Face had played and hunted with slings all their lives. They were both deadly accurate with them.

But Runs With Horses had no desire to fight his father, to try to hit him with a rock.

Red Knife knew his son's thoughts and knew what he must do to change them. With lightning speed he released his sling. The small round rock popped loudly against the bare flesh above Runs With Horses' knee, knocking his leg out from under him and causing eye-closing, breathtaking pain.

Red Knife quickly put another stone in his sling and started to twirl it when a rock struck him in the stomach with a loud thud. He winced and looked in complete surprise at Little Face.

A flash of a smile showed on the boy's face before he had to jump and duck to avoid a rock slung by Stands Alone.

The diversion worked and gave Runs With Horses enough time to get up. He was mad, raging mad, and no longer had any qualms about slinging rocks at his father.

Red Knife released a rock and Runs With Horses turned sideways to miss it. He quickly picked up a stone and with a twirl slung it at his father. The shot was fast and straight, but Red Knife was too quick. He easily jumped over it, and grinned. Now the training would really begin.

A long while later, at Red Knife's command to stop, the four of them dropped to the ground in exhaustion. They had jumped and run, and dodged and slung rocks until their arms hurt and their bodies ached. But strangely, in spite of the great danger or maybe because of it, it had been fun. And no one had been seriously hurt.

Runs With Horses' anger was gone. He looked up and smiled at his father. "I hit you twice."

Red Knife grinned. "I hit you first."

Runs With Horses and Red Knife sat on the rim of a hill, gazing at the plains below. In the distance to the east was the bluish gray outline of the Sierra en Medio peaks and further still, barely visible through the light morning haze, were the Candelaria Mountains.

Red Knife pointed at the En Medio Mountains. "When darkness comes you will go to those mountains. Go across the flats and reach the mountains before the sun rises so you will not be seen. A warrior is there watching for our enemies. Talk to him.

"When darkness comes again, go on." He raised his hand higher. "On to the Candelarias. Do you see them?"

Runs With Horses nodded.

Red Knife lowered his hand and looked at his son. "Another warrior is there. When darkness comes again you will start back and tell us what they said. This is part of your training. You will take no food or water. A warrior must be able to travel great distances quickly.

"When you are in the mountains, stay in the brush. Do not come out until it is dark. Never cross the flats in the day. If you can find no water, get up on a high place and look for green spots. Where the grass is green and the trees grow, there will be water.

"But do not go to it in the day. Your enemies might be there. No matter how thirsty you are, you must not go there until it is dark. Then go and drink."

Red Knife paused, swiping at a fly on his ear.

"Sleep in the day. Even if it is hot, do not go where there is shade. Stay under a little bush in the open or under some grass. Your enemies will look in the shade for you. Do not let them find you there.

"If you are sleeping in the tall grass and you hear a noise, take some of the grass and hold it in front of you and look through it. Unless someone is very close, they will not be able to see you.

"If there is someone far away, and you do not know who it is, find a place that is open but is close to some brush. Make a fire with some grass and put a green branch on it to make smoke. Then put the fire out and hide in the brush. Whoever it is will come and you will see if it is an enemy or a friend. From the brush you can fight or get away if you have to."

Red Knife continued and Runs With Horses listened intently. "If you are lost or cannot find the warrior on the mountain, make a fire and some smoke, then put it out and look around. The man will make one too and you will see where he is.

"If you want someone to follow you, make some smoke and lay down a notched stick pointing in the direction you went."

Red Knife swiped at the fly again. "Do you understand the things I have told you?"

Runs With Horses looked at the scenery below. He wished that his training were over, that he had already achieved manhood. "I understand. Will the next raid be soon?"

Red Knife nodded. "The people need more food, bullets, and blankets. Winter is coming. You will go on the raid. Geronimo has told me this."

The news was good. It would be Runs With Horses' third raid. Only one more remained before he could take his place at the fire with the men.

≈≈≈

Runs With Horses left camp in the dim dusk light, carrying only his quiver, bow, knife, and fire drill. He didn't consider the task ahead of him overly difficult, except for the danger of stepping on a rattlesnake in the darkness or falling into a hole or an arroyo. Mountain lions and wolves could be a problem, but it wasn't likely. Rarely did they stalk or attack people.

The twilight faded into a moonless, black night, causing Runs With Horses' pace to slow. He picked out a star to keep his route straight.

Traveling at night was nothing new. Until a few weeks ago, when his people arrived in the Sierra Madre to hide, to rest, and to make much needed raids on the Mexicans, they had been constantly on the move, doing their best to avoid the Mexican and White Eyes armies who hunted them.

Most of the camp's movements had been at night under Geronimo's leadership. The man had power. He knew things about his enemies that no one could possibly know.

As his eyes became increasingly accustomed to the night, Runs With Horses thought about his life, his people. There had always been raids and war. It was not unnatural. Hadn't the universe been built on conflict, beginning with White Painted Woman and her son, Child of Water, who had slain all the monsters and giants? Lightning and wind continued to quarrel over who was the greatest, as did the moon and the sun. There had never been peace.

For a time, before he grew older and accepted it as a part of life, the bloodshed had troubled Runs With Horses. Many times he'd seen the warriors return from a raid with captives, either Mexicans or whites. With their hands tied behind their backs, the captives were given to the Apache women to be hacked to death with axes and knives as they tried to run away.

Sometimes a boy was brought in and once there had been a girl. At first they were made slaves but later became members of the tribe. One of the small children in camp now was white, and two of the Apache warriors were really Mexicans, captured when they were very young.

But in the last year, angered by being constantly pursued and fearing that life as they knew it was coming to an end, Chief Naiche, Geronimo, and their braves had raided and killed more than ever. Before crossing the border on their way here from Arizona, they'd killed twenty-six whites—mostly farmers and ranchers—and south of the border, some seventy Mexican miners and lonely sheepherders.

≈≈≈

The night and the miles seemed endless. Every now and then Runs With Horses thought he could see the outline of the mountains ahead, but he couldn't be sure. The flats he now crossed were not as flat as they had appeared at a distance. There were many low, rolling hills and at the base of each one an arroyo had been cut into the earth by centuries of flash floods.

The deep arroyos caused Runs With Horses more difficulty than the cactus, which stabbed and scraped his bare legs. The darkness allowed only a few feet of vision, just enough so that he could see the edge of a gully and stop before falling in. If he fell, it could mean broken bones or even death.

Several of the arroyos were too deep and the walls too steep to slide down. This caused Runs With Horses to follow the edge, sometimes for a long while, before he found a place to cross. The detours increased the distance to the mountains considerably.

At last a hint of dawn below the bright morning star in the east exposed the outline of the Sierra en Medio ahead. Runs With Horses stopped, taking his first break since leaving camp.

But his destination was close, and in moments he resumed the same slow but steady jog he'd held throughout the night. Daylight found him high in the brushy foothills of the mountains.

Runs With Horses knew that he might easily spend all day in the brush looking for the brave who was supposed to be there and still not be able to find him. He needed the time to rest in preparation for the next leg of his journey that night.

With that in mind he followed his father's instructions and built a fire, sending up a thick plume of black smoke. He quickly put the fire out and scanned the sky for a reply. Half an hour later he was still looking and about ready to try again when a voice from behind startled him.

"Why are you here?"

Runs With Horses turned, shaken and embarrassed at having let someone get so close without his knowledge. If the man had been an enemy, he'd be dead.

The thin, middle-aged warrior stepped out from behind a tree, a rifle in the crook of his arm.

"Red Knife sent me to find you," Runs With Horses answered. "I am to take back your words."

The warrior stared coldly. "You are a foolish boy. I could have easily killed you. When you make smoke, hide, watch, and listen. You do not know who will come. Our enemies are many."

Runs With Horses' temper flared. The man was, of course, right. But he knew that someday, when the warrior returned to camp, he'd tell the story to the others and they would laugh about it.

"I was looking for your smoke."

The man's expression didn't change. "I made no smoke." He turned to walk away. "Tell him I have nothing to say to a child."

"Wait!" Runs With Horses shouted.

The warrior moved on without looking back and disappeared into the brush. Runs With Horses was hurt and angry. He was proud of his abilities as a soon-to-be warrior. His pride had taken a severe blow.

He started walking, taking long, quick strides. There was no way he could sleep now, not until he calmed down, so he might as well use the time to stay in the brush and circle the mountain. That would put him in a better position at dusk to continue his journey across the flats to the Candelarias.

Besides, he was thirsty, very thirsty. There had to be water somewhere. Food he could do without for another day, maybe two, but water he had to have.

A while later, on the opposite side of the mountain and in the bottom of a shady draw, Runs With Horses stumbled upon a wide shelf of solid rock. In the center were several round holes and he recognized them immediately, having seen them in other places. Red Knife had said that the Pueblos, the same ones who had made the flint arrowheads, had made the holes to collect rainwater.

There wasn't much water, just a little in each hole, but it was enough. His thirst quenched, he moved out of the draw and into a thick stand of tall salt grass. It was a good place to spend the day, he decided, and he lay down in sudden exhaustion, quickly falling asleep.

Several times during the day he awoke and briefly searched his surroundings. At dark he got up and started his trek to the Candelarias. The mountains weren't far in comparison with the distance he'd already covered and he didn't think it should take more than half the night to reach them.

Some time later a faint spot of light appeared in the blackness ahead. Runs With Horses took a few steps forward and the light disappeared. He backed up and there it was again. The light had to be a fire or lantern, which meant someone was there, and the camp was probably in a low draw or swag, where the light could not be easily seen.

Runs With Horses stood still, thinking. He guessed the light to be only a few miles away, but distances were hard to judge at night. If he decided to investigate, it would put him far to the north of his route and add many miles to his trip.

He looked up at the stars. The big cup hadn't turned very much. The night was young and he had the time. Red Knife, Geronimo, and Naiche would want to know who was there and why. But he'd have to be careful. Very careful.

Runs With Horses knew he must be getting close, yet he'd only glimpsed the light twice more since starting toward it. Cautiously he circled the area, wondering if the fire or lantern had been extinguished. If not, whoever it was had gone to considerable trouble to make sure their camp was hidden.

Then he heard voices and saw a dim, reddish glow above the earth some fifty yards to his right. On hands and knees he crawled silently, inching closer on his belly. Below him, in the bottom of a deep, wide arroyo, three men squatted around a small fire, talking in Spanish. One of them took a drink from a bottle and handed it to another, laughing.

Down the arroyo and barely visible, three mules and what looked like a donkey were tethered to the opposite bank. Runs With Horses shifted his eyes back to the men—and the rifles positioned across their laps.

Two of the guns were old Mexican army muzzle-loaders, but one of them was a lever-action Winchester.

At the sight of the Winchester, Runs With Horses' thoughts turned to his father. He pictured himself proudly handing the rifle over to him to replace the one Red Knife had lost.

One of the men below rose, a big, mustached man wearing a wide, floppy, straw sombrero. The man looked up, seemingly straight at Runs With Horses. The young Apache's heart beat rapidly and he buried his face in the dirt, afraid to move—to even breathe.

Finally, unable to hold his breath any longer, Runs With Horses slowly squirmed back from the edge. A burst of laughter came from below and the tension in him eased somewhat. If he'd been seen, no one would be laughing.

Runs With Horses' thoughts raced. He had two choices: Leave in relative safety and continue on to the Candelarias, or stay and risk his life trying to steal the rifle.

The decision didn't take long. The temptation was too strong and the rewards too great. He pictured himself on one of the mules, the rifle in hand, riding into camp.

No, the scene changed. He had two rifles, one for himself and the lever-action for his father. And . . . and there was a mule following behind the one he rode. No, two mules and a donkey.

Runs With Horses smiled. Red Knife would be proud. The entire camp would know of his son's courage, skill, and cunning.

Another thought struck him, a thought giving him more determination than anything else. If he were able to do it, and get away, surely the feat would count for his third training raid, leaving only one to go. His father had said he was to go on the next raid with Geronimo. After that, he'd be finished with his training. He'd be a warrior and could smoke and drink with the men. He could look for a wife.

Runs With Horses moved back to the arroyo edge. When the men went to sleep and their fire died, he must have the location of everything below clearly etched in his mind.

A packsaddle, canvas pack, and three saddles lay in the fringe of flickering firelight. Two shovels and a pick were lashed to the outside of the pack, and Runs With Horses guessed that the men were miners.

On the far side of the fire lay a small pile of broken mesquite branches. Closer to him, beside a large boulder, was a cooking skillet, pot, and burlap sack that probably held foodstuff. Other than a few blankets that had been carelessly heaped on a sandy place and the men themselves, nothing else was in sight.

Runs With Horses studied the men, especially the one holding the Winchester. He was the smallest of the three, a lightly bearded man wearing a dusty black sombrero. The man raised a bottle to his lips and Runs With Horses was glad of it. The more mescal the men drank, the sounder their sleep would be.

He wormed his way back a few feet. There was nothing to do but wait and try to come up with a plan.

At last the men's talk ended and the night was still. As soon as Runs With Horses heard snoring, he inched back up to the edge for a look. The fire was almost out and the men lay side by side in their blankets. Unable to see their rifles, he could only guess that the men kept them close at hand.

Carefully, using senses and skills that had been honed since childhood, Runs With Horses rose and moved ghostlike along the flat until he found a place where he could slip into the arroyo. There he headed for the mules, hoping he wouldn't frighten them.

Specks of still-glowing embers in the campfire ahead warned him he was close. Suddenly an unexpected fear gripped him. This wasn't a game, or training. It wasn't hunting, where the animals couldn't fight back. If anything went wrong, his fault or not, he might be killed.

A mule shifted his feet and though Runs With Horses wasn't close enough to see the animal, he held his hand out to the sound and stepped warily forward.

The vague shape of the animals came into view, their long ears erect. He crept closer, patting the first mule's neck, feeling for a bridle. He untied the reins and let them hang loose over the tether line, then did the same with the other two mules and the donkey. It was unlikely that the animals would realize they were free and leave. When he returned, there would be no time to untie them.

His anxiety was almost unbearable. Now came the hard part of the plan, a plan that really didn't exist.

Somehow he had to steal the Winchester and one of the muzzle-loaders, get the food sack, make it back to the mules, mount up, and ride off leading the other animals, all without waking the men.

The men's snoring was loud and even. Runs With Horses hung his bow over his back beside his quiver and pulled out his long knife. If one of the men did wake up and he had to, he intended to use it.

He crept toward the sleeping men, his tension increasing with every step.

Then he was beside them, just inches from the first man. He recognized the black sombrero covering the man's face. The shadowy outline of the lever-action rifle lay to the side of the man and Runs With Horses gingerly grasped the barrel, pulling the gun slowly to him.

He had it.

One of the men rolled over and Runs With Horses flattened himself on the ground. Everything in him told him to take the rifle and get back to the mules.

But Runs With Horses had never had a gun—had never had the opportunity to get one. And if he missed this one, it might be a long time before he'd have a chance again. The gun would set him apart, give him a status among his people that even a few of the warriors didn't have.

He waited. The snoring continued and there was no further movement. Ever so carefully he worked his way around the feet of the men to the opposite side, hoping to find one of the muzzle-loaders lying exposed like the Winchester had been.

A barrel gleamed faintly in the starlight and Runs With Horses took it in his fingers and gently pulled.

The night exploded. The man lying beside the rifle jumped to his feet and yelled as if ice water had been dumped in his face. The barrel of the second gun was jerked from Runs With Horses' fingers.

Runs With Horses scrambled wildly to his feet and dashed toward the mules, the Winchester gripped tightly in his right hand, his knife in his left. He tripped over something—

and fell. A gunshot roared behind him, further ripping the night apart. With dexterity, and the speed and power that come only from extreme fright, he got back onto his feet at a dead run.

The mules were gone, spooked away by the gunshot. Runs With Horses ran on, knowing that distance and the darkness were his only hope.

He stumbled and fell several more times, traveling faster than his limited vision would allow. Another shot thundered and the men were yelling as he made it out of the arroyo and onto the flat.

Soon his pace slowed. It was too fast, too reckless, and now a greater threat to his life than the men he'd left behind.

Mile after mile Runs With Horses jogged, heading back to the Sierra en Medio. The Candelarias were too far and it would be impossible now to reach them by dawn. If the Mexicans caught their mules and found him in the flats during the day, they'd run him down.

The morning star was bright and Runs With Horses could tell by the gradual incline of the terrain that he was approaching the mountain foothills. He stopped to rest and to fondle the rifle.

His feelings were mixed about what he'd done. Of course, things would be better if he'd gotten the other rifle and the mules, but the gun in his hand was no small prize—and worth every bit of the danger and effort it had taken to get it.

Runs With Horses was sure, however, that stealing the rifle alone wouldn't take the place of one of his training raids. He still had two to go. And the fact that he hadn't gone on to the Candelarias to complete his mission might not set well with his father.

He hoped the gift of the rifle would more than make up for that. Besides, if he had it to do over again, he'd do it the same, except he'd have left the second gun alone and taken the mules.

At dawn Runs With Horses was high in the mountain brush of the En Medio Mountains. Hunger gnawed at him from having gone two days without food, and he was thirsty. The flats below revealed no movement, and he doubted that the Mexican miners would take the time to track him, if they even could.

He stayed in the brush and traveled to the opposite side of the mountain, going to the same spot where he'd smoke-signaled the warrior the morning before. Being called a foolish boy still rankled and he'd thought of a plan to do something about it, hoping to gain food and water in the process.

Runs With Horses made a smoke fire and quickly put it out, then climbed a tall juniper and hid there, watching. It wasn't long before he caught glimpses of the warrior sneaking through the brush. He waited until the man was closer, then levered a bullet into the barrel.

The warrior turned at the sound of the action and Runs With Horses shouldered the gun, pointing it at him.

"You are a foolish man," Runs With Horses said in a loud, even tone. The warrior looked up, finally seeing him.

"I could easily kill you," he continued. "When you see smoke, you must be careful when you approach. You do not know who made it. Our enemies are many."

A smile formed on the warrior's face. Runs With Horses kept the rifle trained on him. "I am hungry. I think you have food . . . and water."

The warrior shrugged. "Come down. I will give you something to eat. Where—what are you doing with a rifle?"

≈≈≈

The following dawn Runs With Horses arrived at camp, going straight to the wickiup he shared with his father. Red Knife sat by a small fire out front. His eyes widened at the sight of the rifle in his son's hands.

"It is for you," Runs With Horses said, proudly handing over the rifle. He could tell by the gleam in his father's eyes and the way the man stroked the receiver that he was pleased.

Red Knife looked up. "What happened? How did you get it?"

Runs With Horses stalled. He reasoned it would be better to tell his father all about it this evening, after the man had gotten used to the rifle and shown it to everyone. Maybe, if he worded the story right, the subject of the Candelarias wouldn't even come up.

"It is a long story and I am tired. Can we talk later?"

Red Knife stood, cradling the rifle in his arms as if it were a baby. "You go and rest. At dark we will talk."

Runs With Horses started into the wickiup but his father stopped him.

"My son . . . "

Runs With Horses turned. Red Knife couldn't get the words out, but his eyes and expression said them for him. In his way, in his silence, he was thanking the boy for the gun.

Runs With Horses smiled. "I am glad you like it."

Runs With Horses was right when he thought the rifle would make up for his not going on to the Candelarias, and wrong when he thought the subject might not come up. But Red Knife was too happy with the rifle and excited at the news of his son's daring exploits for it to matter.

After he'd heard the story, including how Runs With Horses had gotten back at the warrior in the Sierra en Medio, he gathered together as many in the camp as would come and had Runs With Horses tell the story again.

Four days later, at daybreak, Geronimo announced to the camp that the time was right to go on a raid. He'd sung and prayed and the Giver of Life had told him they would have success. He would be leaving at dark.

That afternoon Red Knife was putting paint on his son's forehead and cheeks. "My son, this is your third raid. I will not be going with you. I will stay to guard the camp.

"While you are gone, you must not eat any warm food or you will lose your power with horses; they will not be worth anything to you. Do not eat the entrails of an animal either or the same thing will happen. You must not talk much or laugh, no matter how funny you think something is. If you do, bad luck will come to you."

Red Knife paused, putting a final stroke of paint on his son's chin. He set the bark paint container down and wiped his hands in the dirt. Runs With Horses thought about interrupting his father and telling him that he'd heard all of this twice before, but he decided against it. It wouldn't hurt to listen again.

Red Knife continued. "Do not look up in the sky very much or a heavy rain will fall. You must not go to sleep until you are told to lie down. If you do, you will make everyone in the party drowsy.

"Don't eat much. You cannot eat the best parts of meat. You will eat the tough meat on the neck and the lungs so that the horses will not get tired.

"You must do the work when the party stops to rest. You will take care of the horses, get the wood, carry the water, and do whatever the men tell you. What you do will make it good or bad for the others.

"Do you understand the things I have told you?"

Runs With Horses nodded. And when his father left, he immediately began going through all of his arrows, putting his best ones to one side of his quiver so they could be easily found.

He checked his bow for cracks and was filling the large intestine of a deer with water to take with him when Little Face walked up. The boy's face was streaked with war paint.

Runs With Horses smiled. "I did not know you were going. It is good we will be together."

Little Face sat down, obviously happy. "One

more raid after this one and we will be men. We can go where we want, do what we want. Songs will be sung about us and stories will be told.

"Of all the warriors, we will be the greatest. We will fight the White Eyes and the Mexicans. We will take back our land."

Runs With Horses tied the open end of the intestine shut and threw it across his shoulder. He reflected on Little Face's predictions about the land and knew it would never happen. Red Knife had told him many times that this small band of Chiricahua Apaches was all that was left of the once powerful Apache Nation.

The whites to the north numbered more than the stars. Who could count them? To come here and stay in this refuge was the people's only hope.

The whites and the Mexicans would never be defeated. The most he and his people could hope for was to remain free, free to hunt and to raid—to live as their ancestors had for centuries.

Runs With Horses didn't want to dampen his friend's enthusiasm. He said, "We will go to the horses and make them ready."

The entire camp cheered and clapped their hands as the small raiding party of eight left at dusk, Geronimo riding in front. Runs With Horses and Little Face trailed behind, each of them wearing a buckskin vest the war leader had given them to protect them from harm.

It felt good to be going, to be riding with the men, although both boys knew they would not be allowed to go where there was actual fighting. If one of them were hurt, it would reflect badly on Geronimo's ability to lead. The old warrior wouldn't allow that to happen if he could help it.

Runs With Horses wondered about the rider out in front, the man called Geronimo. For years he'd known him, yet he didn't really know him at all. The man was considered a great war leader and more than once he and his followers had been placed on reservations in Arizona, only to break out again.

Red Knife had said that Geronimo's terrific hatred for the Mexicans started years ago, when he'd returned to camp and found that Mexican troops had killed everyone in it.

Geronimo's mother, his young wife, and his three small children were among the dead.

Others said the story wasn't true, that Geronimo only told it to get sympathy and the truth was he liked war.

Often, when drinking, Geronimo boasted about his seven wounds, and Runs With Horses had heard him tell about them more than once: Geronimo had been shot in the right leg above the knee and still carried the bullet there, shot through the left forearm, wounded in the right leg below the knee with a saber, wounded on top of the head with the butt of a musket, shot just below the outer corner of the left eye, shot in the left side, and shot in the back.

Runs With Horses was sure of one thing—he didn't want to get on the bad side of Geronimo.

As the night wore on, Runs With Horses thought about how riding was much better than walking. He liked the dapple gray horse under him. The animal belonged to his father and Runs With Horses believed him to be Red Knife's best horse. He had a wide chest and heavy quarters packed into a small, chunky frame, which gave him tremendous speed in short bursts and stamina for long distances. The gelding had an easy gait, a responsive mouth, and was gentle enough to be trusted.

A half-moon rose and in its light Runs With Horses watched the gray's ears. A horse could hear and see better than a human at night and he had learned from years of riding that he could benefit by interpreting the animal's ear movements.

If one ear pointed up and the other down, nothing unusual was around. If both ears went up, there was cause for concern. The animal had seen or heard something that interested him. If the horse then stopped, there was definitely something—or someone—ahead.

The miles were uneventful and quiet, except for the occasional howl of a lone coyote and the answer of others in the distance. No one talked and the plodding rhythm of the horses' hooves made Runs With Horses sleepy.

He opened the end of the intestine canteen and splashed a handful of water on his face. He must stay alert. Enemies could come from anywhere at any time, and he must not cause the men to be drowsy.

Daybreak arrived and the party traveled on without rest. Little Face maneuvered his sorrel closer to Runs With Horses. "We have been riding to the north and to the east since we left. Do you know where we are going?"

Runs With Horses shook his head. He noticed the redness in his friend's eyes and guessed that he too had had trouble staying awake. "No. I think only Geronimo knows."

Little Face didn't say any more, aware that he and Runs With Horses weren't to talk very much while on the raid. At midday four specks appeared on the flats in the distance. Moving specks that could be only horses or mules.

Runs With Horses looked at Geronimo and knew he saw them too. The warrior kicked his horse and led the raiding party on in a slow canter. Soon he turned off into a wide, shallow gully, staying in the bed of it.

A long while later Geronimo stopped. The party dismounted and the eight of them crept to the bank of the gully and looked over it. Not far away three men riding mules and leading a pack donkey could be clearly seen. Runs With Horses recognized them instantly. They were the same miners from whom he'd stolen the Winchester.

Geronimo studied the men and their animals. Runs With Horses watched him, having no doubt what the war leader intended to do. A moment later the man backed away from the bank and started for his horse. Runs With Horses followed him, speaking quietly.

"The men. They are the ones I took the rifle from. They still have two old muzzle-loaders."

Geronimo stopped and turned to the youth. Runs With Horses met his penetrating gaze only briefly, unable to look into the cold, mystical eyes any longer. Geronimo slapped him on the back. "It will be easy then."

The party mounted. In seconds they were out of the arroyo and racing across the flats toward their prey. The miners soon saw the danger coming and wildly kicked their mules into a run. But their efforts were futile. There would be no escape, not here on the flats where the horses could easily outrun the mules.

The Mexican leading the pack donkey let him go and the Apache men yelled and whooped, urging their horses faster. Little Face and Runs With Horses were caught up in the excitement, in the blood-rushing thrill of it all, and they started doing some whooping of their own.

The distance was closing and the miners looked back in desperation. A hundred yards further they jumped off their mules, abandoning them and seeking refuge behind a large clump of sand and mesquite.

Geronimo stopped the party just outside rifle range. He looked at the boys. "You will stay here."

He then rode out from the group toward the three Mexicans, his black stallion prancing half sideways. The other braves stayed back, seeming to know what the old warrior was up to and what their part was to be in it.

A puff of black smoke showed above the mesquites, with the simultaneous loud report of a rifle. A bullet struck the ground two horse lengths in front of Geronimo.

Another gun fired and Geronimo let out a shrill yell, running his horse toward the Mexicans. He knew the two single-shot muzzle-loaders were empty and he'd be on them before they had time to reload. The warriors left Runs With Horses and Little Face, quickly joining their leader.

The boys could barely see through the haze of dust caused by the running horses. Three shots sounded in quick succession, more dust clouded around the clump of mesquites, and the air was filled with the frenzied whoops of the warriors.

Twenty, maybe thirty heartbeats and it was over. The three Mexicans were dead. The dust settled and the two soon-to-be warriors could see Geronimo triumphantly holding up a scalp in each hand. He motioned for them to join him.

Bloodshed had been a part of life from the beginning, so Runs With Horses and Little Face were not bothered by the sight of the three bloody, mutilated bodies. Killing your enemies to take what you wanted was necessary, and the Mexicans were the ones who'd started the practice of scalping.

The miners were stripped of their clothes, boots, and hats. One of the warriors held a musket proudly above his head, and Runs With Horses wished he were the one who had it.

After a few of the warriors gathered the mules and donkey, the party resumed their journey. Runs With Horses and Little Face still had no idea where they were going, but the incident with the miners hadn't seemed to alter Geronimo's original plan, whatever that was.

At sunset a single cluster of two or three buildings could be seen to the north. Runs With Horses guessed the place to be a ranch and possibly the reason Geronimo had brought them here.

The weary band stopped for the night in a narrow draw hidden between two low hills. An alkaline dripping-spring was located at the head of it and there was plenty of grass for the stock.

The warriors eagerly took the pack off the donkey and spread the goods out, immediately opening cans with their knives and eating the contents with their fingers. Geronimo picked out a bottle of mescal and sat down to drink.

Little Face and Runs With Horses moved in front of the man, awaiting his instructions. They were as hungry as the others yet keenly aware of the rules for a novice. What they ate and how much of it could affect the success of the raid. The decision was Geronimo's.

The old warrior threw two cans to the youths. "Go stay with the horses. Take turns keeping watch."

Moving up the draw toward the spring where the stock were gathered, they worked to get the animals hobbled and the saddles taken off before it was too dark to see. Afterward, they sat down together to eat.

One can turned out to be peaches, the other tomatoes, and like the warriors they ate with their fingers, sharing their food. The cans were empty much too soon, but at least the edge was removed from their hunger.

Runs With Horses wiped his hands on the grass. "Did you see the buildings to the north?"

"Yes," Little Face answered.

"I think that is where we are going."

"At dawn we will know. You sleep first. I will wake you later."

Runs With Horses lay back on the grass. It felt good to relax his aching body after a night and day of constant riding. Little Face stood and moved further up the hill.

Geronimo roused the camp in darkness. The warriors and the boys hurriedly caught and saddled their horses. There was no wasted motion and in a short time the party moved out, heading north.

Runs With Horses led one of the mules. The other two and the pack donkey followed of their own free will. Soon a dim light in the east warned of the coming dawn.

Geronimo stopped the party and dismounted. He and the warriors huddled together, talking in low voices. A light blinked on nearby and the boys watched it, knowing it came from the ranch. Whoever was there was getting up.

Finished with his discussion with the men, Geronimo stepped in front of Little Face and Runs With Horses. "You will wait here."

The warriors mounted, took the mules, and headed into the desert toward the ranch. Runs With Horses and Little Face stayed on their horses, watching and waiting. As the daylight increased, two low adobe buildings with thatched straw roofs became faintly visible.

A flash, like a low-flying shooting star, hit the roof of one of the buildings. Then came another flash and another. The boys realized what was happening. The warriors were shooting fire arrows. Soon the two roofs were ablaze.

Shots rang out and someone screamed. Then more shots, too numerous and too close together to count. Little Face and Runs With Horses could hear the wild yells and whoops of the warriors.

Then it was over, almost as suddenly as it had begun. Columns of black smoke drifted skyward in silence.

Neither youth spoke. They knew the raid had been successful or the fighting wouldn't have ended so quickly. It wasn't long before the boys saw Geronimo and the warriors racing away from the ranch, whooping in triumphant success and driving a herd of horses in front of them.

As the warriors came closer, it was apparent that the mules now carried large packs of plunder, which had been placed in burlap sacks and tied to their saddles.

Runs With Horses and Little Face joined the band as it passed, quickly helping to push the stolen stock forward. A few of the horses were reluctant to leave the ranch and kept turning back. The boys stayed busy preventing their escape by riding back and forth in the rear.

Further on, cattle could be seen in a wide valley previously hidden by the hills. Geronimo and the warriors spread out and gathered the animals, bringing them in for Runs With Horses and Little Face to ride behind. By the middle of the day, more cattle had been sighted and gathered and the band now held a sizable herd of over sixty animals. There would be no hunger in camp this winter.

Runs With Horses noticed that Geronimo kept looking back over their trail. He thought he knew why. Whoever had been at the ranch early this morning was surely dead, but the smoke from the burning buildings could be seen for miles. If anyone was in the vicinity, they'd investigate, and perhaps they'd follow.

Because of the cattle, the party moved slowly now, leaving a wide trail of churned-up ground. The miles dragged on under the hot sun and a feeling of impending doom grew in Runs With Horses. He wondered if Little Face felt it too.

Sometime later Little Face shouted.

"Look!"

Runs With Horses turned the dapple gray gelding around and looked where Little Face was pointing. Riders were coming, and they were coming fast.

He looked back to see Geronimo forcing his horse through the cattle to the rear, his five braves swiftly joining him. Runs With Horses could guess what was going through the warrior's mind. With the cattle, it would be pointless to try to outrun the riders. There were only four men coming, not enough to cause Geronimo to abandon his plunder.

There would be a fight.

The old warrior gestured with the rifle in his hand at Little Face and Runs With Horses.

"Stay with the horses and cattle." Then he let out a shrill yell and wildly kicked his stallion into a dead run. The braves followed him in a trail of dust.

Little Face edged his sorrel closer to Runs With Horses. Both boys knew that they should turn their mounts around and start pushing the cattle, but they couldn't take their eyes off the two groups of men rushing toward each other.

Suddenly Geronimo and the warriors slid off their running horses, seeking shelter behind bushes, cactus, rocks, or anything that offered protection from which to fight.

A volley of shots echoed and one of the four riders in pursuit fell from his horse. The others quickly stopped and dismounted. Another round of gunfire followed, but it sounded different, further away, and—and coming from a different direction.

Little Face and Runs With Horses turned toward the sound. From the west, in a large cloud of dust, dozens of mounted men were riding hard toward them.

"Soldiers!" Little Face shouted, as much to himself as to Runs With Horses. "It is the Mexican army."

Runs With Horses looked back to where Geronimo and the braves were fighting. Obviously they too had seen the new danger, for they were running, trying to catch their horses. Shots rang out and one of the warriors tumbled headfirst to the ground.

"What do we do?" Little Face cried out.

Runs With Horses looked at the fast-approaching army. He realized there was nothing he and his friend could do to help Geronimo and the warriors. If they took the time to try, the army would be all over them. He knew the livestock and plunder were lost. They'd be lucky to escape with their lives.

"We run!"

To the east a deep arroyo blocked their way. They followed the edge of it south only to find that the arroyo turned back to the west—toward the Mexicans.

There was no choice, no other place to go. They'd have to jump it.

Runs With Horses put the gray into a full gallop, grateful for the horse's power. Little Face followed some distance behind on the sorrel.

The gelding continually picked up speed and Runs With Horses leaned forward as far as possible, laying his head against the animal's neck. He'd jumped arroyos on horses before, but none so wide as this one.

A final mighty thrust and the gray flew through the air, landing on the other side with just inches to spare. Runs With Horses pulled the horse to a stop and looked back in time to see Little Face's sorrel stumble at the edge and fall headlong into the deep gully.

The Mexicans were close now and Runs With Horses faced the hardest decision of his life. Should he ride on and save himself or go back for his friend, who more than likely lay at the bottom of the arroyo, crushed to death by the weight of the sorrel?

A rifle boomed and a bullet kicked up dirt a few feet from Runs With Horses. His thinking stopped. He leaped from the gray, wrapped the rawhide reins once around a greasewood limb and rushed to the edge of the arroyo. He had to try, had to do something.

Little Face was standing in the bottom, clawing at the steep bank for a root or anything that would help him climb out. One of his legs was twisted to the side, obviously broken. The sorrel stood a few feet down the arroyo, trembling.

Runs With Horses removed the bow from his shoulders, dropped to his stomach, and reached down with his bow as far as he could.

"Little Face!"

The boy looked up, his face raw from the fall. He strained to reach the bow with both hands.

Runs With Horses felt the impact of a bullet strike the ground by his left foot. He scooted his chest further over the arroyo edge, lowering the bow even more.

Little Face jumped on his good leg and grabbed the end of the bow. The sudden jerk of his weight was almost more than Runs With Horses could hold.

"Climb!" Runs With Horses yelled, knowing that if he shifted from his position and tried to pull his friend up, he'd fall in himself.

Hand over hand Little Face climbed up the length of the bow, then up Runs With Horses' arm like it was a rope. When Little Face reached the top, Runs With Horses let his bow drop and grabbed his friend under the arms, swinging him up and over the edge.

The Mexicans were shouting and a rolling, thunderous volley of shots sprayed lead around them. With enormous effort Runs With

Horses slung Little Face over his shoulder and ran to the gray, setting his friend on the animal's back.

Bullets continued to whistle through the air and Runs With Horses marveled that neither of them had been hit. It had to be because of the protective vests Geronimo had given them. Of that, he was sure.

He pulled the reins free from the limb and swung on behind Little Face, instantly kicking the gray into a run. The horse seemed to want to leave the roar of the guns as badly as they did and ran with all his might.

Runs With Horses looked back. Several of the mounted Mexican soldiers were lined up at the arroyo's edge, shooting at them, but none dared to try to cross it. In seconds the gelding carried the boys out of rifle range. They had made it. They would live to go on their fourth and final training raid.

Gunfire continued to sound behind them and Runs With Horses wondered about Geronimo and the warriors.

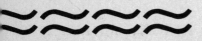

Runs With Horses and Little Face rode the gray gelding throughout the evening, the night, and most of the following day before arriving at camp exhausted and half starved. Little Face's leg was swollen to twice its normal size and the youth was in terrible pain. They'd seen no sign of Geronimo and the warriors.

Everyone in the camp surrounded the boys, wanting to know what had happened. Little Face's mother gave him a mixture of herbs to drink and between bites of venison and mesquite bean bread, the boys told their story.

Afterward, Red Knife and Chief Naiche took four hot coals from the fire and placed them on Little Face's broken leg. The boy winced and gritted his teeth. Along with the herbs, the charcoal was to kill the pain and to help reduce the swelling.

The leg was broken below the knee. Red Knife placed a hand on each side of the break. Naiche pulled on Little Face's foot while Red Knife jerked the bones in place. Little Face screamed, then lay still. He was unconscious.

≈≈≈

Runs With Horses sat beside his father in front of their wickiup. He had just gotten up and the sun was already high. He felt good. The food and the many hours of needed sleep had revived him.

He looked at his father. "How is Little Face?"

"He is fine. But it will take long for his leg to grow together."

Runs With Horses gazed at the wickiups nearby. The camp was quiet today. Unusually quiet. None of the children were playing and only two women could be seen outside cooking.

"Geronimo?"

"He and two braves are here," Red Knife answered.

"Two braves?"

"The others will not be coming back."

Runs With Horses turned to his father. "Then there will be a war dance. A war party will go out to punish our enemies."

Red Knife shook his head. "There will be no dance, no war party. Long Nose is in the flats with his scouts and soldiers. Tomorrow Naiche, Geronimo, and the other men will meet with him at the banks of the Bavispe River."

It took Runs With Horses a minute to remember that Long Nose was the name the Apaches had given Lieutenant Gatewood. The white, lanky, long-nosed lieutenant had been in command of the Fort Apache reservation in Arizona Territory. He was one of the very few whites his people trusted and considered a friend.

"Why has he come?" Runs With Horses asked. "We are in Mexico. He has no power here."

"The Mexicans and the whites to the north have joined together to fight us. Long Nose brings a message from the general of the white army, a man called Miles: Surrender, or he will hunt us until the last man, woman, and child are dead."

"Geronimo will never surrender," Runs With Horses said excitedly, getting to his knees. "We will not go back to the reservation to starve and be treated like dogs. We are free. We will stay free."

Red Knife shook his head. "It is over. Everyone is our enemy. We have no friends. This very mountain where we hide is against us. It is a shield that also holds us prisoner. There is no place we can go.

"The Apache scouts who are with Long Nose told us that the White Eyes have taken the families of Naiche and a few of the other warriors off the reservation in Arizona and put them in a place far away called Florida. Naiche misses his wife and children. He will surrender and go to them."

Runs With Horses' thoughts raced. From the time he was big enough to walk, in one way or another, he had been disciplined and trained to fight, to become a warrior. One training raid remained and the lifelong goal was his. Without that raid, he would never be considered a real man. He couldn't take his place among the warriors or participate in the war dance. He couldn't marry and raise a family.

He glared at his father. "Geronimo is not a coward! He will not give up. He will fight until the end."

Red Knife looked at his son a moment before speaking. "He will stop fighting. He has surrendered before. The people are against him. They say he has lost his power. The raid cost six horses and three warriors. Nothing was gained."

"And you," Runs With Horses almost shouted. "What will you do?"

Red Knife stood. "Do not raise your voice to me. I have told you before. The whites are more than the stars. Now they have joined with the Mexicans. We cannot win. We cannot hide where they will not find us.

"This"—he gestured at the camp—"is what is left. The whites have taken our land. Our lives are all we have. If we do not surrender, our women and children will die for nothing."

Runs With Horses got to his feet and looked at the sky. His voice was softer. "You have said many times that your son will be a mighty warrior. Tell me, who will I fight on the reservation where they will put us? What good are the things your father taught you and you have taught me? Can you tell me this?"

Red Knife looked at the ground in silence. He had no answer.

Runs With Horses stood a few feet from Little Face's brush wickiup. Following Apache custom, he coughed and cleared his throat, letting anyone in the shelter know he was there.

"I am here," Little Face said. "Come in."

Runs With Horses pulled back the deer-hide door, bent down, and stepped in. As in his own home, only a small amount of sunlight penetrated the brush walls and it took a moment for his eyes to adjust to the dimness. Little Face lay to the side on a blanket.

"Your mother is gone?" Runs With Horses asked.

"She is out to look for some roots, plants, and seeds. She thinks they help me." He chuckled.

When Runs With Horses didn't smile, Little Face could tell something was wrong. He reached across his blanket and lifted up his bow and arrow-filled quiver. "Here," he said. "I want you to have this."

Runs With Horses stood still. He knew that the bow was Little Face's most precious possession and a full set of arrows took a month or more to make. The gift was not a small one.

"I—I cannot . . ."

"Take it." Little Face raised the bow and quiver higher. "You lost your bow in the arroyo. You saved my life. You will have it."

He patted his broken leg. "I have time to make another bow and set of arrows."

Runs With Horses knew that if he persisted in refusing the gift he would offend his friend. He moved beside Little Face, took the bow and quiver, and sat down.

He wondered how he was going to tell Little Face that it didn't matter, that where they were going they wouldn't need their weapons except to hunt, and game was always scarce on a reservation.

Little Face watched Runs With Horses absentmindedly run his fingers along the bow. He hadn't seen his friend look so sad since the day his mother died.

"What is it?" Little Face asked. "What has happened?"

Runs With Horses was silent a moment. Then slowly, and with several heated interruptions from Little Face, he told about the discussion he'd had with his father. Little Face rolled to the side and tried to rise up on his good leg. Runs With Horses stopped him.

"What are you doing? You cannot walk. You will hurt your leg."

Little Face strained against Runs With Horses' hold on his shoulders. Sweat beaded his forehead. "I will be a warrior like my father! I will fight and be free."

"No!" Runs With Horses shook his friend. "You will die. You cannot win. Everyone is our enemy. We have no friends. It is over."

Runs With Horses stopped, astonished that he'd used his father's words. Anger rose in him at how quickly he too had given up. There had to be a way for him and Little Face to become men.

His mind whirled. Suddenly he drew a deep, steady breath. "We will be warriors. We will go on many raids together. No one will be able to stop us. We will leave the reservation whenever we please and take much booty to spread among our people."

Little Face relaxed and Runs With Horses released his hold.

"Songs will be sung about us," Little Face exclaimed. "Everyone will know of our courage and daring."

A smile spread across Runs With Horses' face. "The White Eyes and the reservation cannot stop us. Of all the warriors, we will be the greatest."

EPILOGUE

Geronimo, Chief Naiche, and a few warriors met with Long Nose (Lieutenant Gatewood) on the banks of the Bavispe River. Gatewood's message from General Miles was brief: "Surrender and you will be sent to Florida to rejoin your families; after two years you will return to the reservation in Arizona. Accept these terms or fight it out to the bitter end."

After a day of discussions and following Lieutenant Gatewood's advice to trust the general, Naiche and Geronimo agreed to surrender to Miles at Skeleton Canyon in Arizona, but they would keep their guns. The White Eyes had lied too many times.

On September 3, 1886, General Miles met the Apaches and promised them protection from their enemies, reunion with their families, and a large, well-stocked reservation, all of which were conditions he knew would not be honored.

The small band of thirty-eight Apache men, women, and children accompanied Miles to Fort Bowie where they were disarmed by a large force of soldiers, put in wagons, and hauled to the Bowie Train Station as prisoners of war. Miles quickly sent a message to the War Department stating that the band of Chiricahua Apaches had surrendered unconditionally.

The Florida-bound Apaches were loaded into railroad cars. As the train started to roll, several Apache scouts who had gathered to see the train off were disarmed and treacherously thrown in boxcars to become prisoners like the rest. For years the faithful scouts had helped the United States Army fight against their own people and this was how their loyalty was rewarded.

Geronimo and Chief Naiche repeatedly took turns voicing their regret at having listened to Gatewood and General Miles, but it was too late. The fate of the last free Apache band was now sealed.

The train stopped in Texas and for two months the prisoners were held at Fort Sam Houston while their plight was further discussed in Washington.

President Cleveland finally made a decision that struck the cruelest blow yet to the Apaches. The Apache men were to be separated from their families and held at Fort Pickens on Santa Rosa Island in Pensacola Bay; the women and children were to be sent to Fort Marion, Florida.

A month later the War Department ordered all Apache boys and girls between the ages of twelve and twenty-two to be sent to the U.S. Industrial School at Carlisle Barracks in Pennsylvania to be taught to live like white people. There, the boys' hair was cut and they were forced into shirts and trousers, the girls into dresses.

The Apache people, unaccustomed to the humid Florida climate and given inadequate clothing and shelter, suffered from exposure and disease. Many died of malaria or tuberculosis.

Those Chiricahuas who survived the harsh conditions were held by the United States government as prisoners of war for the next twenty-seven years, never again to return to their homeland.

BIBLIOGRAPHY

The following books were used in research for this novel and provide much fascinating and useful information.

Ball, Eve. *In the Days of Victorio.* Reprint, Tucson, Ariz.: University of Arizona Press, 1970.

Barrett, G.M. *Geronimo's Story of His Life.* Interpreted by Ace Daklugie. New York: Nuffield & Co., 1906.

Betzinez, Jason, and Wilbur S. Nye. *I Fought with Geronimo.* Harrisburg, Penn.: Stackpole Co., 1959.

Lockwood, Frank C. *The Apache Indians*. Reprint, Bison, Nebr.: University of Nebraska Press, 1987.

Opler, Morris E. *An Apache Life-Way*. New York: Cooper Square Publishers, 1965.

Reedstrom, Lisle E. *Apache Wars: An Illustrated Battle History*. New York: Sterling Publishing, 1990.

Worcester, Donald E. *The Apaches: Eagles of the Southwest*. Reprint, Norman, Okla.: University of Oklahoma Press, 1979.